Please Don't Tickle The Tiger

Written by Ryan Cedar

Illustrated by Dawnna Jean Pearson

ISBN-13: 978-1495497568
ISBN-10: 1495497569

To Boo, Daazy, and Dodo,

You make my heart happy whenever you smile

—*Dad*

Contents

Marshmallow Trees

I wish there were marshmallow trees,

That grew in great numbers with ease.

That's a tree I could hug

With my hot chocolate mug

As I waited for each passing breeze.

Did You Know...?

Mice love to fly kites but you don't usually see

When their miniature kites get stuck in a tree.

The strings are so tiny, the kites are so small,

And the mice don't go get them for fear that they'd fall.

You almost never see them in flight

'Cause your cat is awake

So they fly them at night.

Clowning Around

I tied a balloon to my toe, just for fun,
Then one on another, and thought I was done.
But that made me wonder just what it would do,
If I made it four instead of just two.

Well, I looked kind of silly with only the four,
So I blew up some others and added six more.
One on each toe, 'til I felt like a clown,
There's only one problem now... I'm upside down.

Time to Go

Mom says if I don't get out
I'm going to be sorry.
The sun went down,
She's leaving soon,
The sky is getting starry.

But here I am, swimming still
'Cause I'm still having fun.
I have no plans
To leave the pool—
I will not miss the sun.

She says that if I don't get out
I'll turn into a fish.
Well, that's just fine
'Cause you know what?
I'll finally get my wish!

Try Counting Peanuts

Elephants have trunks on their heads,
And that's why they don't sleep in bunk beds.
'Cause their trunks would hang over so slumpy,
That the guy on the top, whose snoring won't stop,
Would make the poor guy on bottom quite grumpy.

Buzzy

There was a little bee named Buzzy.

His eyesight was blurry and fuzzy.

It took him an hour to find one pretty flower

'Cause he never knew where he wasn't or was he.

Not a Hair Brush

Hedgehogs are cute and cuddly and kind,

But they are NOT good for brushing your hair.

They are sweet, they are neat, they can tickle your feet,

But they are NOT good for brushing your hair.

If You Listen Carefully

Hummingbirds can fly upside down, that is true

And they are not much bigger than your thumb.

They can squeak, they can chirp,

They can chatter and cheep,

But I've never heard a hummingbird hum.

Not Scary

There was a terrible creature who lived in a cave

And he only came out once, at night.

But the moon was so shiny,

And he was so tiny,

That he ran back inside with a fright!

I Scream For Pancakes

I'm screamin' for pancakes,

I'm shoutin' for eggs

And I'm yellin' while smellin' my toast.

But I am shakin' for the bacon

That you started makin'

'Cause that is the one I love most.

It's Snow Trouble

There's no day like a snow day,

A "Stay-Home-From-School-And-Go-Snow-Play."

But snow is cold and wet,

A fact that I often forget,

'Til it gets in my pants,

And I do the "Snow Dance"—

When I shake it all out in my own way.

If I Were a Tree

If I were a tree, not a thing would be neater,
Than smelling myself as a Western Red Cedar.

If I were a maple, the finest of Europe,
I'd start every morning with pancakes and syrup.

And if I were an apple tree, that would be grand,
'Cause I'd eat all the fruit from the palm of my hand.

But... if I were a Redwood, you know what I'd like?
For kids to come see me and go on a hike.

A Bad Idea

There's an awfully big tiger named Tickles,

And he lives in a cage at the zoo.

But some kid was curious,

And made Tickles furious—

Now a sign tells you what to not do.

What I Wished For

I had a rough time at school today
'Cause the bullies were picking on me.
They stole my lunch,
And took my shoes,
Then threw them way up in a tree.

But, on the way home, I found a lamp with a genie,
And he said, "There's no need for your sorrow.
I'll grant you one wish."—
And that's just what he did.
And now I can't wait for tomorrow!

Sleep Over

I have the neatest pet at home,
The rarest of his kind.
The problem is, when he gets loose,
He's very hard to find.

He's crafty and he's cunning,
He's clever and he's keen,
And when he sneaks around the house,
He's almost never seen.

Did I mention that he's very small,
And sometimes he will bite?
Are you still coming to my house,
And staying overnight?

I Wouldn't Do That If I Were You

Be careful when you make a frown,
Don't linger when you're sad,
Use caution when your chin hangs down,
And tiptoe when you're mad.

The Grouchy Monster sees that stuff,
And that's what makes him come.
Did you just hear that "Huff" and "Puff"?
Oh, please don't suck your thumb!

Well, it's too late now, my dear,
I see he's getting nearer.
And if you don't believe he's here—
Just go look in the mirror.

The Strangest Thing

Every night at our house there's an odd transformation:
Something so strange, it defies explanation.
The circumstances, it seems, are really quite sad.
The only person affected so far is our dad.

He says he can't help it, he loses control.
He makes silly faces and then his eyes roll.
He shakes and he growls, without reason or rhyme,
Except that it happens every night at bed time.

Mom shouts, "Run! Hurry! Get in your beds!
Pull up the blankets and cover your heads!
The Tickle Monster won't get you
'Cause you're safe when you're sleeping.
Close your eyes tight—he can see if you're peeking."

I guess Mom is right 'cause it works like a charm.
He never does tickle or do any harm.
If it's a disease then I hope we don't get it.
And if dad is faking—he sure won't admit it!

And Now You Know

In an old western town, when times were still rough,
There was a cowboy named Willy, who thought he was tough.
He growled at the folks as they passed, walkin' by.
If he looked at a baby, the baby would cry.

With only two teeth and a big lower lip,
He drooled as he walked with a gun on his hip.
The meanest of pranks he would do just for fun,
And he did all them things with his little squirt gun.

They had a sheriff named Jim—he was the best of the best,
And they sent him for Willy to make an arrest.
He rushed to the saloon, with a plan in his mind,
But sadly "Wet Willy" snuck-up-from-behind.

He pulled out his squirt gun, just as he drew near,
And quietly placed it... right next to Jim's ear.
"The rest," they say "is history."
And now you know the mystery.

Not So Fast

'Tis a pirate's life for me, my friend,
And I'll sail the seven seas—
To look for buried treasure then,
And go wherever I please.

I'll sing all day and laugh and play.
Me mates and I will sail away.
We'll eat like kings with golden rings,
And dance with chance for better things.

What's that, you say? Put down my sword?
And take off my silly hat?
There are no kids allowed aboard?
Well, of course I didn't know that!

I have never been viewed with such attitude
And don't you know, sticking your tongue out is rude?
Fine! Go sail the sea, I'll head home for tea—
And my lost-treasure map, you'll never see!

Imagination

A book is a magical thing—
Hidden treasure inside,
You will find
If that sense of adventure
That lives in your heart
Were set free
With the key in your mind.

~The End~

Made in the USA
San Bernardino, CA
23 February 2014